Dan Anthony

Dan began writing for children as a scriptwriter for the BBC's Tracy Beaker series. His books are funny, sometimes a bit scary, and always full of surprises. 'The world isn't boring,' he says, 'it's completely crazy – but for some reason grown-ups keep going on about the dull bits.'

Huw Aaron

Huw is a cartoonist and illustrator whose scribbles have appeared in hundreds of magazines, comics and books. Monsters and aliens are his favourite things to draw ... but pirates are also pretty cool!

Steve's Dreams

Steve and the Singing Pirates

First published in 2015
by Firefly Press
25 Gabalfa Road, Llandaff North, Cardiff CF14 2JJ
www.fireflypress.co.uk

Text © Dan Anthony 2015
Illustrations © Huw Aaron 2015

A CIP catalogue record of this book is available from the British Library.

Print ISBN: 978-1-910080-32-0
Epub ISBN: 978-1-910080-32-7

This book has been published with the support of the
Welsh Books Council.

Typeset by: Mad Apple Designs

Printed and bound by: Bell and Bain, Glasgow

Steve's Dreams

Steve and the Singing Pirates

by
Dan Anthony
illustrated by Huw Aaron

Firefly

1

Music

That morning I woke up suddenly, as if some kind of alert had sounded. I jumped up and checked the area through the skylight 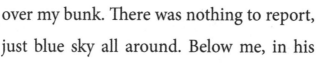 over my bunk. There was nothing to report, just blue sky all around. Below me, in his bunk, my little brother, Kyled, was on the wriggle, burying himself deeper and deeper under his Incredible Hulk duvet. He was the one who woke me up. I stuck my head over the side of my

bunk and looked down. I could see a lump moving under the Hulk.

'You can run, but you can't hide, Kyled,' I said. Kyled hated getting up.

Kyled stopped moving. Now he was playing dead. The oldest trick in the book.

When I reached the kitchen, Mum was already dressed. She checked her watch before pouring hot water on her instant coffee.

'Where's Kyled?' she asked.

'Hiding,' I said, taking my blue bowl down from the plate cupboard.

'Where?'

'In his duvet,' I said, putting in the cereal. I poured some milk on.

'I'm going to get him now,' said Mum. 'Don't forget it's Mrs Gestetner this afternoon.'

I bowed my head. I'd been trying not to think about it. I knew I had Mrs Gestetner at 4pm, but so far I'd avoided the thought.

'It's the holidays,' I said. 'She's probably not working.'

'She is,' said Mum, hurrying past. 'She says that if she doesn't keep teaching students in July and August they take four steps backwards. I want you to practise while I sort Kyled out. We have to go out this morning.'

I pushed my cereal around in its blue bowl as Mum hurried upstairs. The thought of Mrs Gestetner worried me. I hadn't practised and I hated her lessons. She made me feel like a boy with no talent.

Just then I heard a huge cry coming from upstairs. Mum had found Kyled. There were crashes and bangs. The kitchen ceiling shook. The plates in the plate cupboard rattled as Kyled roared and ran from bedroom to bedroom. I could hear my sisters Jaydee and Miffany stomping after him, screaming at the tops of their voices.

Then it stopped. That could mean only one thing. Mum had pinned Kyled to the floor. Now the screaming and shouting started. That could mean only another thing. They were getting Kyled dressed. He was only four, but he had the strength of a grizzly bear. I winced at the noise as Miffany pulled a T-shirt over Kyled's head.

I finished the last soggy bits of my cereal and went out into the hall.

Mum came downstairs holding Kyled by the hand. His face was red. His hair was brushed. He was wearing an Incredible Hulk

T-shirt and red shorts, he had his best Ben 10 socks on and his new orange trainers.

Jaydee and Miffany stood at the top of the stairs in their dressing gowns, waving.

'Don't worry, Kyled, you won't be too long in LoSave,' said Jaydee.

'Then you can come and watch us.'

Kyled grinned. Miffany and Jaydee had entered themselves in the Pendown's Got Talent competition at the Bastion Cleverly Leisure Centre. Jaydee and Miffany were going to sing and dance. They'd been practising their song for ages. They'd even created a name for themselves: The Piratellas.

I went out into the back lane to kick the ball at the spot. I hadn't been doing it for long before Toby joined me. I'm not sure why he likes hanging around with me. I'm nine, he's thirteen.

'Hi, Steve,' he said. 'What you doing?'

'Spot on,' I said, kicking the ball.

He watched the ball. It hit the spot, bounced back into the lane and rolled to the drain. You get double points for a direct hit from the drain, because it's hard to get your foot under the ball. It generally means you can't get the height to hit the spot.

Toby lined up his shot. He was going for a flick, scooping the ball up with his toe so that it ballooned through the air and touched the spot on the way down – a tricky shot for a good footballer. For Toby it was almost impossible.

I say 'almost' because we all know that nothing is actually impossible. Or to put it another way, anything is possible.

Toby tried his flick. He mistimed it. The ball flipped out of the drain and rolled depressingly along the tarmac. It didn't even reach the wall.

'Are you going to watch The Piratellas?' he asked.

'Actually, Toby, I'm not,' I said. 'I live with

The Piratellas. That's quite enough.'

Toby surprised me sometimes. He should have understood that the chances of getting me to go down to Bastion Cleverly Leisure Centre were non-existent. The place gives me the creeps. When I was small I got my toe stuck in a trampette at Sean Griffith's sixth birthday party. The leisure centre reminds me of bad things that happened in the past.

'I can't go, anyway,' I said.

'Nerves?' asked Toby.

'It's unmentionable, it's an unmentionable thing,' I said.

'What is?' asked Toby.

I looked at him. He seemed to expect an answer.

'How can I possibly say?' I said. 'It's unmentionable, that means it cannot be mentioned.'

'You can tell me,' said Toby. 'Is it something really bad? Is it another dream? You're always going on about dreams?'

'I've got a piano lesson,' I said.

I thought about piano lessons and shivered. I would have booked tickets for The Piratellas if it had meant missing my piano lesson. Even though she was little, there was something powerful about Mrs Gestetner. She gave me the creeps. For example, when I put my fingers on her piano keys I always thought she was going to smash the cover down on them, chopping them off. That's the kind of lady she was: flowery dress and cakes in the morning – de-fingering in the afternoon. You could see it in her eyes – her glasses made them look huge, like an alien's. If she caught your eye and looked at you, you felt as if she was staring through your eyes, down the string that ties them into your head. She was pulsing beams directly into your brain. The best thing to do was never to look into her eyes.

'D'you want to come down the rec?' I asked.

Toby looked at me. Nobody ever asked him to come with them anywhere. He was one of those kids who spends a lot of time on his own. He was wearing jeans, a T-shirt with a photograph of a pelican on, which he'd had scanned on from a school trip to a bird sanctuary, and a LoSave baseball cap. Not one you can buy, one you get given if you work there. His uncle worked in LoSave. Toby loved LoSave, he said it had everything you could ever want in the whole of your life.

'Err, yeah,' he said. 'Are you sure?'

'Come on,' I said, 'so long as you don't talk about music.'

Of course he didn't listen. He kept going on about how great my sisters were.

'You see,' he said, as if I didn't get it, 'pirates are usually boys. But "....ellas" makes you think they're girls, right?'

'I get it,' I said. 'Look, Toby, it's just my sisters, Miffany and Jaydee, wearing lots of stripy pirate clobber, dancing around and singing their ridiculous song.'

'I really dig their song,' said Toby. 'Man.'

I sighed. There was no doubt about it – Toby was an actual fan of my sisters. I tried to get him to talk properly, but it didn't work.

We reached the rec. Two teams were getting ready for a baseball game. I could see the bases being set up. In the background kids were playing cricket and kicking footballs around. There was one guy, probably a student, throwing a boomerang.

As Toby talked, we watched it fly high into the blue sky, then zoom around in a circle, looping back behind the guy who threw it, before hovering a few yards away from where he stood.

I'd seen boomerangs before – I remembered my last dream. I thought about telling Toby about it, but when I added it all up – stepping out onto the roof of my house in the middle of the night, jumping off the tiles into the floating 'Library of Dreams' that looked like the church where Mum takes her Spanish lessons, meeting Big Mo and the other librarians and then discovering that this was the place where all the dreams ever created were kept – I decided to leave Toby out of it. He was thirteen. They say that's a difficult age. The dream stuff could have completely freaked his mind.

'You know what?' said Toby.

'What?' I asked. Although I wasn't really listening. I was checking out the park. I looked back towards the library. Everything seemed normal. But something told me we were being watched. The next time I scanned the park the boomerang, and the guy throwing it, had disappeared. I had a strange tingling in my spine, the hairs on the back of my neck spiked up. Big Mo was about. I knew it. Another dream was coming.

'I can play the piano,' said Toby, 'I can help you practise if you want.'

I shook my head.

'You can't play the piano,' I said.

'I started on the piano,' said Toby. 'I wasn't very good, so they put me on the trombone.'

'Great,' I said, 'so really what you're saying is that you can play the trombone. It doesn't even look like a piano.'

'I'm saying I started on the piano. I can do some stuff. I can help you.'

2

The Boomerang

Toby and I arrived back at my house just as Mum pulled in. Kyled was sitting in the back on his booster seat. He had a punnet of strawberries in one hand. When he saw me and Toby he stuck his tongue out.

'I'm a bit concerned about Kyled,' I said as Mum opened the door for him. 'I don't think we should be giving him too many treats.'

'Hi, Steve,' said Mum, as Kyled clambered out. 'Glad to see you've found a friend.'

Kyled rushed towards the house.

'Kyled was so good,' said Mum.

'What did he do, Mrs James?' asked Toby.

'Errr, there's no need to call my mum Mrs James,' I said. 'You can call her Tiffany.'

'Actually,' said Mum, 'Mrs James will do fine. And, since you ask, Kyled was very good in the supermarket. He didn't even ask for sweets, so I bought him strawberries for a change.'

I've got a keyboard. Mum borrowed it from school for me to practise on. In the beginning everybody was satisfied with the arrangement. The school was pleased because they always say in my reports that I should join in more; Mum was happy because she thought playing the piano would let me prove to people that I was good at something and Mrs Gestetner was chuffed because she got the money for teaching me.

In fact the whole deal didn't suit anyone. All the other kids at school who might have been good at piano were deprived of a turn on the keyboard; I was terrible at playing and I hated going to Mrs Gestetner's. Far from making me feel confident and gifted, a half hour with Mrs Gestetner made me a cucumber-fingered dork boy. It wasn't doing anything for my self-esteem.

I decided that this time the lesson was going to be different. By transforming Toby's special trombone skills, I'd prove to them all that I was a great musician. I took Toby and Kyled up to the room at the top. I plugged the keyboard in and told Kyled to sit on his bunk.

He nodded. He seemed docile. Perhaps his behaviour was improving. Soon Kyled had nodded off on the bottom bunk, leaving

Toby and me time to learn the piano
properly.

'Play something,' said Toby.

'Play something?' I asked. 'Are you crazy? I'm still on learning the notes.'

I showed Toby my book: *The Piano For Beginners* by Wolfgang Amadeus Lofthouse. He may as well have called it: 'I can do it – you can't – byeee.'

Toby opened the book. To my surprise, he folded the pages back and began to play a tune on the keyboard. He could understand the dots on the long lines. He could read keyboard music.

'I thought you played the

trombone,' I said.

'I started on the piano,' he said.

'But they took you off,' I said.

'It doesn't matter, once you can read trombone music you can read any music.'

'No way,' I said.

'Way,' he said.

'I thought it was different for every instrument – are you saying that trombone music looks the same as other stuff?'

'Yes,' said Toby.

'Wow,' I said.

'Now,' said Toby, 'put your hands on the keyboard and look at these notes. Everything starts with the middle C.'

'Surely it should start with A?' I said. 'That's the first letter. Music should go from A to Z.'

'There's no Z sharp,' said Toby. 'At least I've never heard one. It's A to G beginning with C.'

I was getting confused. Why start music with a C when you've already got an A?

Just then Kyled woke up. He was sick all over the keyboard. Then he fainted. I ran downstairs as fast as I could. I found Mum, Jaydee and Miffany in the kitchen straightening their hair.

'Mum,' I yelled.

This time I went with Mum. Toby was sent home.

We sped out of our estate, past LoSave, onto the Western Distributor Road and then off at the medical centre roundabout. Mum kept looking behind us at Kyled. He sat in his seat, his face was white, and he could hardly keep his eyes open.

I didn't know what to say to Mum. I

couldn't say, 'Don't worry, it'll be alright,' because I thought that it wouldn't be alright. Perhaps Kyled had been poisoned. I shook my head as I watched him.

'Don't worry,' I said to Mum. 'We can get some kind of monument put up.'

Mum looked at me out of the corner of her eye.

'Try to pay attention to the road ahead,' I said. 'I appreciate how stressful this is.'

She swung the car into the health centre. While she parked and grabbed Kyled, I ran on ahead. 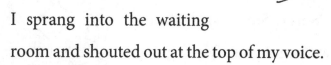 I sprang into the waiting room and shouted out at the top of my voice.

'Emergency! Poisoning coming through.'

Then Mum rushed in carrying Kyled in her arms. The nurses were waiting for her. They took Mum and Kyled straight into one of the doctor's rooms. The waiting room was quite full. Everybody looked at me. I didn't quite know what to do. So I sat down, picked up one of their magazines and started reading.

I expected to find myself waiting in there for ages. But within a few minutes Mum appeared holding Kyled's hand. He was walking. His skin had gone less pale and blotchy. The dark rings under his eyes had disappeared.

Mum and Kyled walked through surgery out into the car park. Then they came back.

'Sorry, Steve,' said Mum, 'we forgot you. Kyled's going to be fine.'

'It was an allergic reaction,' she said. 'Kyled's

allergic to strawberries. They make him drowsy, nauseous and blotchy. They gave him an antihistamine and now he's getting back to normal.'

'Good,' I said, following them to the car. 'So Kyled will survive after all.'

Mum gave me another one of those looks.

Kyled snored in his booster seat behind me.

When we arrived back home, Jaydee and Miffany needed Mum to help them in the kitchen with their nails, their hair, their make-up, their shoes and their clothes. I went upstairs to clean Kyled's sick out of my keyboard. Guess what? After I'd rinsed it out thoroughly it didn't work.

3

Mrs Gestetner

It was three o'clock. Showtime.

Jaydee sat in my seat at the front. Mum drove. I sat behind her next to Kyled and Miffany sat next to him. Jaydee and Miffany were wild with excitement. They kept singing their song and going through their moves. Jaydee and Miffany had given themselves a kind of pirate look. Jaydee had a stripy shirt and long false eyelashes. Miffany had piled her ginger hair up on her head into a huge beehive, and she wore long boots and a pirate's jacket.

I lent forward as Mum pulled out of our street.

'Mum,' I said, 'if you'd like me to show some support for Jaydee and Miffany, I don't mind coming to the Bastion Cleverly Leisure Centre to watch them sing.'

She sighed. 'I'm dropping you at Mrs Gestetner's, then we're going to the concert.'

'I'm just saying,' I said, 'I think I'd actually quite like to see the performance.'

'Don't start, Steve,' said Mum.

'Don't start what?' I asked.

'It's a piano lesson. You don't want to go. You'll say anything to get out of it.'

'Mrs Gestetner is an evil brain destroyer, you have no idea what happens to me when I step over her threshold.'

'She's a piano teacher, Steve, not a Dark Lord.'

'I'm telling you, if I wasn't a strong individual with a good grasp of right and wrong, she'd have turned my head towards the ways of the underworld by now,' I said.

'Steve,' snapped Mum, 'if you were supportive of your sisters you wouldn't be talking about yourself now. You'd be giving them encouragement.'

I thought for a while as we drove out of our estate and onto the dual carriageway that led to the Bastion Cleverly Leisure Centre roundabout.

'I like the song,' I said to Jaydee and Miffany as they sung. 'Has it got an A in it?'

Mrs Gestetner's house is in a cul-de-sac called Melody Court, a little way away from the Bastion Cleverly

Centre. We pulled up at the
end of it. Mum didn't want to
drive down because it wasn't
easy to turn the car around.

I stepped out, holding my music book and
Mrs Gestetner's money envelope.

'I'll be back in an hour,' said Mum. 'If I'm
late, tell Mrs Gestetner to put you in the
garden.'

They drove off.

I looked at Melody Court. It was similar
to our street except the small brick houses
were gathered around a little turning circle.
Mrs Gestetner was always looking through
her curtains to make sure that people didn't
park on the circle. Everybody who lived on
the circle liked to keep an eye on it, to stop
the circle parkers. Mrs Gestetner's house
was at the far end of the circle. As I walked

across it, I could feel the eyes of all the people who lived around the circle. I knew they'd be checking me out. They didn't like strange cars parking on their circle and they hated strange people wandering into their circle. Any stranger who came into the circle was likely to be trouble for someone. The people in Melody Court didn't like trouble, strangers or parkers.

I walked up to the front door of Mrs Gestetner's house, which was on the side of the building. I pressed the bell. Tingly bells, like sleigh bells, chimed out inside.

The door opened and Mrs Gestetner poked her head around it. She blinked at me through her big glasses. I took a step back, horrified at the piercing nature of her enormous dead eyes.

'Ah, Steve,' she said, holding out her bony blue hand.

I placed the money envelope into her hand and she let me in. I followed her down the thickly carpeted hall into the piano room. I sat on the stool in front of the piano. Mrs Gestetner sat beside me on her stool.

I put my book on the music holder.

'Ah,' said Mrs Gestetner. 'Wrong again, Steve.'

'But I haven't done anything yet,' I said.

'We don't start with Wolfgang Amadeus Lofthouse, do we?'

'I know,' I said. 'I was just putting him on the music holder ready for when we do.'

'I've got a new piece,' she said, standing up. Mrs Gestetner's piano stools were like boxes: you lift up the bit you sit on and find sheets of music underneath. I think Mrs Gestetner thought this was cool. Probably to her, the idea of a seat you could keep music in was like the idea of a mobile phone that could access YouTube and Facebook: two apps in one piece of hardware.

As she rummaged around her chair, I looked around the room.

The walls were white, the carpet was grey, the window looked out over the empty cul-de-sac. Pictures of former pupils hung on the walls with captions underneath. I read one of them – a fat boy wearing a gown and flat hat was holding a rolled-up certificate: Snooks Creamer – Certificate of Merit – International Pianists' Federation. A little further down the wall was a girl standing next to a piano wearing a purple prom dress:

Pansy Jenkins-Jones – National Keyboard Institute Award For Excellence. And then in a really big frame was a studenty-looking guy with thick glasses and a strange centre-parting haircut. This was Mrs Gestetner's pride and joy: Mostyn Reginald Victor Norris – First Class Honours – Performance Piano, Newport Conservatoire of Performing Arts.

'Ah, Mostyn,' said Mrs Gestetner, slotting her music in place above the keyboard. 'I see you have spotted M. R. V. Norris. He really was a special one.'

'I know,' I said.

'By your age he was playing Mozart's Piano Concerto number 21 so well that it used to make me cry.'

I shifted in my seat. I didn't know whether Mrs Gestetner meant that if I could make her cry through my piano playing that would be a good thing or a bad one.

'He looks good,' I said, nodding towards the picture of Mostyn. 'Like he means business.'

'Oh, Mostyn,' said Mrs Gestetner again. 'There will never be another Mostyn. Now, Steve, are we ready for "Pigs' Trotters"?'

'What?' I asked.

Mrs Gestetner nodded towards the music. The new piece called 'Pigs' Trotters'.

'It's very simple, very basic, it sounds like pigs' feet — it's good for boys like you, who find it difficult to bring a sense of rhythm to their music.'

I looked at the rows of black blobs on their long lines. I hadn't quite got used to what notes the blobs meant. I tried. I pressed a key.

'Wrong,' said Mrs Gestetner.

I tried another.

'Wrong,' said Mrs Gestetner.

I tried another.

'Honestly,' she said, 'have you any idea what you are doing?'

I shook my head. I couldn't speak. I felt so angry with Mrs Gestetner – I mean, I was there because I didn't have any idea what I was doing. I was supposed to be finding out.

'It's a C,' she sighed.

I pressed the C that Toby had showed me.

'Good,' she said.

I relaxed.

'And the next note.'

I stopped relaxing.

In the end Mrs Gestetner said that I hadn't been practising, that I didn't have any sense of rhythm and I would never make even a quarter the piano player that Mostyn

Victor Reginald Norris of the Newport Conservatoire was. I told Mrs Gestetner that she was a weirdo witch living in a cul-de-sac full of curtain-twitching zombies. She opened the piano stool and stuffed a sheet of music into my hand. She said Mostyn Norris could play this when he was two. Then she said I couldn't go into the garden, which was just as well because she probably stuffed it full of the bodies of the ones who didn't get the reason why music starts on the third letter of the alphabet. I felt her eyes eating my brain and dived under the piano stool covering my eyes with my hands. I shouted that it was ridiculous that everything begins with C. It should be begin with A.

Mrs Gestetner kind of quivered; her blue eyes fixed me with a death-ray glare, I avoided it by staring at her reflection in the photograph of Mostyn the Magnificent holding his awards.

'I think you've said quite enough, you had better leave,' she whispered.

I ran out of her house to the top end of the cul-de-sac and sat on the sign pointing down to Melody Court. The day was going badly. I tried to add up the problems. There were so many of them that I began to cry. Not like a baby, more like a person who's got too much stress.

Problems:

- Kyled had been sick in the school keyboard – now it didn't work.
- I'd washed the keyboard – that meant it was my fault.
- Mrs Gestetner would tell Mum I'd been bad – I'd probably get grounded.
- I wasn't where I was supposed to be. Mum liked me to be where I was supposed to be – she wouldn't like finding me not in Mrs Gestetner's garden.
- Music begins with the third letter of the alphabet – this makes no sense.
- If I got grounded I'd be stuck in the house with Kyled – this would be terrible.
- If I didn't get grounded I'd be stuck outside with Toby – that would be terrible.
- Dad would be told about Mrs Gestetner – he was working in Khazakstan on the oil rigs, but he'd still go mad.

Possible Problems:

- Dad might get so mad with me he'd make a mistake and blow his rig up.
- This would cause serious trouble. For a start, we'd all have to go to Khazakstan to make sure he was OK.
- An international incident might be triggered off, causing a big war.

The more I thought about it the longer the list got. There was one other thing. While I was sitting on the Melody Court sign I looked up into the sky, the way people do when they've got a lot of problems. I saw a seagull flapping across the blue sky, or what I thought was a seagull. It came closer and closer until I realised, almost too late, that it wasn't a bird. I had to duck to avoid it and it clattered onto the pavement beside me.

It was a boomerang. I picked it up. There was a message, written on the back of the boomerang in black ink.

'To Steve, from the library – HELP.'

There was no doubt about it. Big Mo was after for me. Strangely, I felt almost relieved to get the message.

After a long wait, Mum arrived in the car. They were all in it. I climbed in the back and did my best to explain what had gone wrong. Nobody seemed to care. Jaydee and Miffany had won the singing competition. They really were musical. Pendown loved them and the Bastion Cleverly Leisure Centre had gone mad when they sang their song:

We are the Piratellas,
We sail the seas and blow up fellas.
We take their boats and steal their treasures,
And sing all day and dance all night.

They had been entered into the regional final which would take place in Newport, at the Riverfront Centre. Everybody loved the Piratellas.

But my mind wasn't on the music. As they sang their song over and over again, I was thinking about something else. What did Big Mo want? What was going on up in the Library of Dreams?

That night I climbed up the ladder, lay on my bunk and stared up at the skylight over my head. Gently, so as not to wake Kyled, I sat up. Through the skylight I could see stars and planets appearing high above the orange glow of Pendown. I reached up and pushed the skylight open. I saw the archway floating in the black sky just like last time. I could just about make out figures hurrying back and fore in the flame-lit hallway of the Library of Dreams.

Outside on the roof I could feel my feet slither on the damp, dewy tiles. This time I didn't hesitate. It had been such a bad day I didn't really care about the possibility of sliding down the roof and crashing into the garden. I took a step forward into the air.

4

The New Mission

A hand clamped down on Steve's shoulder. It was Big Mo. Grey hair shot out from the sides of his pork-pie hat and he smiled broadly. All around the librarians hurried backwards and forwards wearing their hooded robes, ferrying books from the racks that twisted far away into the distance.

'Welshy!' said Big Mo. 'How's things in Wales?'

'It's Steve,' said Steve. 'And I live in Pendown.'

Big Mo gave Steve a look and guided him through the forest of stone towers wrapped in wooden staircases which climbed up the towers like ivy.

'Hard to remember and difficult to find – just the way we like it,' said Big Mo. 'Good to see you. Glad you got the message.'

'On the boomerang?' said Steve. 'You could have taken my head off.'

'I thought it was a neat idea. I have to say, rescuing the last Neanderthal baby in your first dream, using nothing more than a paperweight borrowed from the correspondence section of this library seemed pretty impressive to us. There's no way you'd let a little stick with a message on give you any trouble.'

The lanterns lighting the library crackled and spat. Steve could see the head librarian's little wooden office in the distance.

'Are you sure?' asked Steve.

'People up here think you're pretty cool.'

'People down there think I'm a fool,' grumbled Steve.

Big Mo pushed the door to the office open. The librarian was sitting behind his desk just like the last time. His brown

robe and hood made it difficult for Steve to see his face. Behind him, on the notice board, he and Big Mo had written staves of music and notes.

'Know anything about this kind of stuff?' asked the librarian, jabbing his thumb at the board.

Steve looked at the notes, then the librarian, then Big Mo.

'Is it a tune?' asked Steve.

The librarian nodded, he seemed impressed.

'I'm more of a blues man myself,' said Big Mo. 'Two or three chords, a howlin' guitar and boy, can I sing the blues. But when it comes to dots on pages — I must confess I get a little lost. Steve's the man for the job. Give him the equipment.'

The librarian stood and handed Steve a

neat pile of clothes. On top of the pile was a cat, curled up in a deep sleep. Big Mo picked the cat up and stuck it on Steve's head. Steve jumped and tried to pull it off.

'It's a wig,' said Big Mo. 'Calm down.'

Then the librarian handed Steve a small stick. Steve thought it looked like a wand. He pointed it at the librarian's desk and tried to turn it into a bunch of flowers.

'It's a conductor's baton,' said the librarian. Now get changed quickly – we've got an eighteenth-century emergency for you.'

'Isn't that the time of pirates?' asked Steve as he changed into a long jacket, trousers that only came down to his knees and a pair of boots with huge buckles on them. 'Can I be a pirate?'

'If we need to help a pirate, we'll be in touch,' said Big Mo. 'For the time being, it's a musician who needs our help.'

'Use the wand, sorry, baton,' said the librarian opening the door at the back of the room. 'It'll help you.'

Steve looked sadly at his baton.

'This is just a stick,' he said.

'Good luck,' said Big Mo, holding the door open to a small empty room with white walls, a wooden floor and a window looking out onto a street.

'Wait a minute,' said Steve. 'Who am I trying to help? How will I find them? What do I do?'

Big Mo's hand came down on Steve's shoulder. Before Steve could react he found himself forced out through the door.

'Wait!' shouted Steve. 'I'm not ready.'

But it was too late. Steve tumbled into the room. 'Wigs,' he muttered, as he moved to the window for a closer look. Everybody outside, the men, the women, even the children, were wearing wigs. Steve rubbed his eyes. In the distance he could see a lady wearing a huge pink dress, with a wig like

white candyfloss on her head, walking her dog. Even the dog was wearing a wig. Or perhaps the dog had had his hair cut to make it look like he was wearing a wig.

Steve listened to the sounds of the old city. Gradually over the constant clop of horses' hooves on cobbles and the grinding of cartwheels a new sound crashed into his ears. Strange, harsh-sounding music blasted down onto the street. Somebody was practising an instrument. They weren't very good. To Steve it sounded worse than The Piratellas.

'Will you be quiet!'

From inside the house a gruff voice echoed upwards. Steve span on his heels and hid behind the door.

'Shut it!'

And again.

'So help me, if I have to come up there I'll slice that thing up into strips with my cutlass then blow you to smithereens with my blunderbuss.'

Steve's ears pricked up. Whoever was shouting sounded to Steve like he might know something about pirating after all.

5

Wolfie

A bell tinkled outside Steve's room. He pushed the door open and edged into a hall. There was no one around. If he could get to the front door he might find out what was going on.

Steve crept on tiptoe, towards the front door. In the corridor, ticking loudly, was a grandfather clock. Steve tried to time his footsteps with the ticks, but the wooden boards still creaked as he crossed them. Steve noticed a couple of wooden crutches resting against the side of the clock. Then he heard the noise again. Crashing down the staircase from the top of the house was the strange, horrible music. It sounded really bad, thought Steve, much worse than when he practised.

He stopped in his tracks. Now he could hear a new sound. The staircase descended below ground level and someone, or something, was grunting and puffing their way up. Steve shrank back from the hall, back into the empty room. He watched through a crack between the door and its frame.

A small man, wearing a huge scraggy ginger wig, with a wooden leg and patch over one eye stumbled up into the corridor from downstairs. He hobbled to the front door, picking up his crutches as he went. Steve could see the jewel-encrusted handle of a long sword sticking out from under his coat.

The man pushed the front door open to reveal a crowd of people. A young woman with an angry look on her face shouted from the front.

'Will you tell whoever it is that keeps playing that damned harpsichord at the top of your house to stop it,' demanded the woman. 'Day in day out, in the middle of the night, first thing in the morning, none of us can get any sleep. It's keeping my baby awake.'

'The worst thing is,' said a tired-looking man at the back of the crowd, 'it doesn't change — it's the same old song over and over again. After a while it does things to your mind … terrible things. I CAN'T STAND IT ANY MORE!!!!'

A big man in a black coat, with a bald head and a gold earring, produced a pistol from inside his jacket.

'I say we just go up and shoot the varmint,' he added. 'I'm not a violent man, but after three days of listening to that racket, it's him or me. Either he shuts up, or I shoot him or...'

The man thought for moment. Then a rather tired look of realisation crossed his face.

'Or I shoot myself.'

He held the gun to his own head.

The man with the wooden leg held his arms up. He waved his crutch, silencing the crowd.

'Alright, alright, I'll see what I can do. But

remember, Wolfie is a tenant. He rents his room fair and square. So long as he coughs up the dough once a month I'm not going to pick a fight.'

The music stopped.

Everybody looked around.

A bird tweeted.

Then, just as the neighbours sighed with relief, it started again. A terrible discordant racket crashed down to the street from a room high above them in the rooftops.

'That's it,' said the man, pulling back the firing pin on his pistol.

'Wait,' shouted the man with one leg. 'I'll see what I can do.'

He span around on his wooden leg and stepped back into the hall, slamming the front door behind him. He swung himself towards Steve's door. But he didn't open it.

'Oi, mush.'

Steve gulped. The man appeared to be talking at him.

'Yeah, you,' said the man peering through the crack before shoving the door open with his crutch.

Steve stared at the man. His wig was almost the same size as his body.

'Get up to the top room. Tell Wolfie if he don't shut up he's going to start a riot. Emphasise the fact that if he don't desist playing that loathsome tune of his, one citizen of our district will feel compelled to blow his own brains out as a means of extracting himself from the infernal noise. And if that don't work, you could mention the fact that I'll be up there with Slicer if he wants to take things any further.'

And, with surprising agility for an old-looking fellow in a ginger wig with one leg, the man slid his silver sword from its scabbard and swished the air with it.

Steve gulped again. He could hear the sharpness of the blade as it cut the air.

'T … t … top flat,' he stammered.

'Yeah,' said the man, replacing his sword, 'then we'll talk about what you've come to see me about.'

Steve looked blankly at the man in the huge wig. He had no idea what he'd come to see him about.

'Lodgings,' said the man. 'Rooms. You'll be wanting to know what rooms I've got on offer and how much a month's board is. You'll be wanting to see the accommodation.'

Steve nodded and rushed up the stairs.

The building was tall and thin, the staircase seemed to go upwards forever. On each landing there were two doors. Most were closed, but some were open. Steve could see that almost every room was occupied. At the very top of the staircase, right under the roof, there was a low door. Steve tapped on it and stepped into a tiny room.

A young man sat at the keyboard of an instrument that looked like a very old piano. Steve hesitated.

'Err, sorry to bother you, Mr, ummm, Wolfie,' said Steve. 'But they're asking you to stop. They're begging you to stop.'

'Never.' The man hit the keys and began playing again.

The sound was terrible.

'STOP!' yelled Steve, bringing the keyboard lid down with a crash, just missing Wolfie's fingers.

Wolfie pulled his hands away. Steve guessed that Wolfie was young, about eighteen years old. He was skinny and pale, wearing the same kind of clothes as Steve. A jacket, weird knee-length trousers, big buckled shoes and a completely ridiculous brown wig that looked like a rat hat. Steve looked at Wolfie. There was something strangely familiar about him. Maybe it was the wig, or the jacket, or the fact that he kept playing the same song over and over again, but there was something about Wolfie that reminded him of his sister, Miffany. He remembered how excited she was as they drove to the Pendown's Got Talent competition.

'It's terrible,' said Wolfie, interrupting

Steve's daydream. 'I've been trying for days to compose a tune, and I just can't do it. I get so far into it and then it stops.'

Steve looked at the keyboard.

'It's a harpsichord,' said Wolfie. 'Haven't you seen one before?'

'Oh yes,' lied Steve. 'My brother was sick in one of these.'

Wolfie scrutinised Steve. He noticed the baton in his hand.

'I see you carry a conductor's baton,' said Wolfie. 'You're a little young to be a conductor, unless, of course, you're a child prodigy.'

Steve smiled. He nodded, although he didn't know what 'child prodigy' was.

'Can you help me?' asked Wolfie.
He pulled a grey handkerchief out of his pocket and blew his nose. Then he started to cry.

'I'm sorry,' blubbed Wolfie. 'You must think I'm a terrible fop. I just get emotional. I keep telling myself it's normal, musicians are known to be emotional sorts. But this problem is simply too much for me. You're a musician. You understand what it's like.'

Steve swished his baton around.

'Yeah,' he said 'I get a lot of problems when I'm doing my conducting stuff. I don't cry though. Well, I don't cry much.'

Wolfie sniffed. He looked up, straight into Steve's eyes.

'I'll tell you – but first, please, say you'll help me?'

'Of course I will,' said Steve. 'It's what I'm here for. I think.'

6

The Captain

Steve and Wolfie hurried down the long staircase. Wolfie's story was incredible and Steve knew that being cooped up in the room at the top of the house wasn't going to help him. They'd reached the front door and were just about to step outside into the street when Steve felt something tugging at his leg. He was hauled backwards across the shiny wooden floor.

Steve looked up. A familiar face, with a brown eye, a ginger wig and a scar across one cheek peered down at him.

'Just what exactly is your game, Mr…'

'Steve,' said Steve.

'It's all right, Captain,' said Wolfie. 'He's with me, he's a friend.'

'You two boys had better come with me,' said the Captain, unhooking his crutch from Steve's leg. 'There's nothing that can't be fixed over a glass of grog.'

The Captain led the boys downstairs to his 'rooms'.

In fact the Captain, who owned the house, lived in one room. It was really a kitchen, with pots and pans hanging from the walls, a fire glowing in the hearth and, all around, seafaring equipment. Harpoons, chests, even an old canon were strewn around the room. Thick Persian carpets covered the floor and in the middle of the room was a dark polished

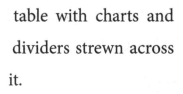

table with charts and dividers strewn across it.

'The Captain was a privateer,' said Wolfie, 'a long time ago.'

Steve's jaw dropped. He'd never met a pirate before.

'Pleased to make your acquaintance, Steve,' said the Captain. 'You like my pad? Thirty years in Totuga, Barbados, the East Indies, Bermuda, privateering for the English crown. Look what it gets you.'

Steve spotted a huge shark's jaw hanging over the fireplace. The Captain had used the teeth to hang strings of onions off.

'A pile of rubble,' laughed the Captain, pouring himself a drink. 'In a town called Newport.'

'I invested my haul of treasure in real estate,' he said. 'Now I have a house full of tenants and my mission is to stay put and look after the rent. Are you going to join my crew, Steve? A shilling a month, washing taken in on Thursdays, breakfasts for an extra four pence and once a year we go on a house trip out to the park to see the peacocks. It's hardly rock and roll, but it beats dying on the boards of some broken shipwreck with a bullet in your chest.'

Steve explained that he wasn't interested in a room.

'Then what are you interested in, Steve?'

'Music,' said Steve.

The Captain laughed: he loved old sea shanties — especially the rude ones.

'The Captain's a wonderful fellow,' said Wolfie. 'He's murderous, he's stolen a lot of treasure, but he's kind at heart. He lets me stay here for nothing so long as I help out with the breakfast.'

'Did I tell you how I lost my leg?' said the Captain, sipping his grog.

'He goes on a bit,' whispered Wolfie to Steve.

The Captain nodded towards the shark's mouth. It was big enough to stand in.

'Ran into some Frenchies off Devil's Island. There were three ships in the line. They blew us out of the water. Found myself floating with sharks – that one decided to have a go at my toes.'

The Captain pulled out a dagger from inside his jacket and flung it at the shark's mouth. It embedded itself in an onion, hanging right in the middle of the mouth.

'Who do you think came off worse?' asked the Captain, with a glint in his eye. 'He got a leg, but I got the fish and chips.'

'Well,' added Steve, 'if that's all you wanted to say, then Wolfie and I had better be off. Thanks for everything.'

'Not so fast,' said the Captain. 'You don't think an old pirate ever forgets the taste for adventure, do you?'

The Captain stuck out a finger, he wiggled it in the air, then he sucked it.

'My senses tells me you pair are about to set sail on a new adventure.'

Wolfie shook his head.

'No,' said Steve. 'We're not adventuring. Wolfie's a composer and I'm a conductor. Could we be any more boring?'

Steve pulled out his baton and waved it around.

'I don't use swords,' said Steve. 'I use weedy little sticks. We don't need swords and ships. You'd be really bored hanging around with us two.'

The Captain looked at Steve.

'I'll be the judge of that,' said the Captain. 'Have you any idea how dull it is in the property rental market?'

The Captain tapped a chest with iron bands on it. He flipped it open with his crutch.

'Empty. You spends the treasure too quickly in this life,' said the Captain. 'Mark my words, Steve and Wolfie — you spends the treasure too quick.'

'We've really got to go,' said Wolfie.

Steve and Wolfie made for the staircase leading up to the hall.

Steve stopped. He heard the hissing sound of a sword being drawn from its scabbard. He turned and was met by the tip of the Captain's blade, pushing very gently into the skin on his throat.

'This isn't an order,' said the Captain, 'but if you don't tell me what's afoot and let me help you, I might be forced to create a little adventure of my own here.'

7

Wolfie, Liam and The Countess of Shropshire

The Captain led Steve and Wolfie through cobbled streets to what Steve would have called a café, but the Captain insisted on calling a coffee house.

'Three double grande lattes with no extra sprinkles,' he snarled.

The Captain adjusted his wig as he sat down at the table. He was waiting. Steve spoke, slowly and carefully.

'This situation has to be handled with skill and intelligence,' he said.

The Captain nodded, his brown brow furrowed, and his eyes went slitty and wily looking.

'I'm with you, boy. We'll wait for nightfall, we'll sneak up behind them and then we'll cut their throats.'

Steve ignored the Captain.

'Wolfie is a musician,' he said.

Wolfie nodded.

'Not a very good one,' said the Captain.

'He's been commissioned by a young aristocrat called Liam to write a beautiful piece of music that will win the heart of a beautiful young woman: The Countess of Shropshire.'

'Shiver me timbers,' said the Captain. 'I've seen her in the papers. She's a looker and no mistake. They do say she's got more wigs and shoes than there are wigs and shoes in the whole of France and believe you me, those

Frenchies like their wigs and shoes. I've never seen a wiggier or shoeier bunch.'

Steve interrupted the Captain.

'The Countess has organised a competition between two rivals for her hand,' said Steve.

'Liam and Earl Mostyn must present her with a piece of music – the one she likes the best wins her hand in marriage,' added Wolfie.

'My goodness,' said the Captain, draining his coffee. 'I can see what the problem is –

your tune is frighteningly bad, Wolfie. People would rather end their lives than listen to it. Whereas Earl Mostyn's will be excellent. I've heard of him too. He owns a huge house just outside town, he's got money, land and prospects. It's a no-brainer. The Countess of Shropshire should marry Earl Mostyn. Liam is wasting his time. The fact that people say Earl Mostyn's an obnoxious and precocious young buck who looks down on everyone he meets is of no consequence. Take the pirate's way – follow the money. '

'We're on Liam's side,' Steve pointed out.

'Oh dear,' said the Captain. 'What can Liam give the Countess of Shropshire that Earl Mostyn can't buy?'

'A song,' said Steve. 'It's a song contest. Liam and Earl Mostyn are going to present their songs to the Countess at 7pm this evening, down by the riverfront. She'll choose whoever brings the best song.'

'That's where I come in,' said Wolfie. 'I write the songs.'

'You see how important it is for Wolfie to practise? If he can't get his song right, Liam will lose the competition and the Countess of Shropshire will marry Earl Mostyn,' said Steve. 'Now, Captain, do you know anywhere safe we can send Wolfie – he needs to practise.'

With a sudden movement the Captain pulled a dagger out of his belt and nailed it deep into the tabletop.

'I've got the very place for a happy

harpsichordist to hone his harmonies,' he snarled. 'Make no mistake, nobody will dare to disturb us where we're going.'

They stepped warily onto the deck of the old ship. Above them fraying ropes and tattered sails flapped in the breeze. Below decks, fat rats groaned as the sound of boots on rotting boards broke their afternoon naps.

'This is my old ship,' said the Captain proudly. '*The Black Dragon* is in a sorry state. She's rotting on a mudbank half a mile from docks. But what can I do? There's no money in pirating today. You're far better off investing in real estate.'

The Captain pushed the door and led the way into his old cabin. Steve and Wolfie followed. The room was furnished in just the same way as the Captain's kitchen at home. Old rugs lay on the floor, dusty charts and rusting dividers were strewn over a large table and, on the wall, they saw another shark's mouth – bigger than the last. The Captain nodded towards it.

'Fell overboard on the Barbary Coast,' he said. 'Wrestled that one with one arm tied behind my back.'

The Captain moved to the side of the room and flipped open the lid of a keyboard instrument.

'There you go Wolfie, try this. It was made for the King of Spain by the best craftspeople on the Spanish Main. Write your tune on that. Nobody but the rats will hear you playing out here.'

Wolfie ran his fingers up and down the keyboard. It sounded much better than the one he had at home.

'Get writing,' said Steve to Wolfie. 'The Captain and I will be back in a couple of hours. We've got to speak to Liam.'

8

Explosions

Steve thought that Liam looked very grand in his white jacket with gold trim and his white shoes with gold buckles. Liam was standing near the big bay window in his living room, leaning on a silver-tipped cane, staring at a letter which he held in his shaky hand. He had big brown eyes like a frightened deer. Steve looked around the room. There was a huge fireplace, great pictures on the wall and, strangely, a big carved pelican in the corner.

'This is a disaster,' said Liam, mopping his brow with a huge spotted handkerchief. 'I so do not dig this. Man.'

'Listen, Liam, I know we've just met, but do you mind if I ask you a personal question?' asked Steve.

'Fire away,' said Liam.

'Have you ever met, had anything to do with, seen from a distance or read about a person called Toby. Tobes to his friends?'

Liam scratched his head.

'Who?' asked Liam.

Steve sighed with relief. He didn't mind hanging around with Toby in real life but he didn't see why he should be allowed into his dreams.

'I'll explain,' said Steve. 'I've just been with your composer and the music is going to be fantastic. The Countess of Shropshire will hear it, fall in love with it – then you.'

'That's if I live long enough to hear the tune myself,' said Liam.

He handed the note to Steve.

dear Liam,
I do challenge thee to a DUEL
yours sincerely,
Egel Mosly
xx

Steve began to read. Liam cast an eye over the Captain.

'Who is this hairy-looking character you've brought with you?' he asked.

'An old sea dog, Sir. He accompanies me on all my adventures,' said Steve, not taking his eye off the page. 'They call him the Captain.'

'You are a musician too?' asked Liam, turning his attention to Steve.

Steve was still reading. But he remembered the conductor's baton sticking out of his pocket.

'Yes, you could say that. I know a few notes,' said Steve.

'Well,' said the Captain. 'What does the note say?'

Liam stepped towards the window and clasped his hands behind his back.

'If only things weren't so complicated – first she wants a song, then she wants a song contest and now this,' said Liam.

'Earl Mostyn has challenged Liam to a duel,' said Steve. 'He says he'd rather blow out his brains in the park with a gun than do the same thing with a trombone on the riverfront.'

'Excellent,' said The Captain. 'I likes the cut of this Earl Mostyn's jib.'

'He's not on our side,' said Steve. 'Earl Mostyn is a big-headed bully. I've come across him before.'

The Captain apologised for getting

mixed up.

'Liam,' asked Steve, 'are you any good at duels?'

'Never been in one in my life. I'm a lover not a fighter,' said Liam sadly.

'Then we shall have to step into your back garden and practise,' said the Captain, producing two large pistols from inside his jacket. Steve was amazed at the amount of weaponry the Captain managed to conceal in his clothing.

In the garden they placed a flowerpot on top of Liam's sundial. As they walked away from the pot the Captain loaded the pistols.

'The rules are simple,' said the

Captain. 'You each take a walk for twenty paces and then when the referee drops a handkerchief to the floor, you shoot one another. The winner is the one who doesn't die.'

They stopped and the Captain handed Liam a loaded pistol. Liam looked at the flowerpot.

'Keep your hand steady,' said Steve. 'You need to squeeze the trigger gently.'

Liam fired. Steve grabbed his ears. The pistol sounded like a hundred fireworks going off at the same time. White smoke filled the garden. But when it cleared the flowerpot stood, undamaged, on the sundial. Steve handed Liam another gun.

'Have another go,' he urged, as the Captain began reloading.

BANG. Liam fired again. This time the

bullet flew upwards and smashed into an upstairs window, shattering the glass.

'Not bad,' said Steve. 'But we've got to get closer.'

'Don't worry,' said Liam. 'I'll get the hang of it.'

Liam tried again but Steve could see the barrel of the gun moving around in little circles. He watched as Liam closed his eyes and squeezed the trigger.

When the smoke cleared, the flowerpot on the sundial was still in one piece.

'Perhaps it would be a good idea if you kept your eyes open,' said Steve. 'When you do the shooting part.'

'He's a dead man,' the Captain muttered, adjusting his wig. 'Couldn't hit a whale from three feet.'

Steve kept handing reloaded pistols to

Liam, and Liam kept missing the target. Steve realised that Liam would be shot if he fought the duel against Earl Mostyn.

9

Duel In The Park

It was him. Just like he looked in the photograph, but bigger, more supercilious, and with a slimier smile.

Earl Mostyn wasn't like Liam. He sat astride his huge black stallion, twiddling the curls of his enormous shiny black wig beneath a vast oak tree – waiting. A footman positioned a few yards away held a blood-red cushion carrying two shiny new silver pistols.

'Be sure, Footman,' he was saying, 'when the duel

commences you hand the gun on the right to Liam and the gun on the left to yours truly.'

When he saw Liam, the Captain and Steve approaching, Earl Mostyn leapt off his horse and swaggered towards them.

'I thought you weren't going to turn up,' he said, pulling off one of his black gloves. 'At least you're not a coward, you're merely a fool.'

'I've been practising like mad,' said Liam. 'You're the one who's going to look silly.'

'If silly is riding off into the sunset with the most beautiful girl in the world, whilst you lie dead in the park for crows to feed off – then silly it is,' said Earl Mostyn. 'Chose your weapons.'

'Actually,' said Liam. 'I won't be fighting this duel today.'

A fiery look crossed Earl Mostyn's face. He stepped up to Liam and slapped him across the face with his glove.

'What do you mean? Are you a coward, Sir? Have you come all this way to tell me that you are about to run away, squire? Are you even sillier than I first thought?' said Earl Mostyn.

'Not so fast,' interrupted the Captain. 'According to the rules of duelling, Liam is entitled to appoint a second to do his shooting for him.'

The Earl looked down at the Captain. In comparison with the fine clothes and muscular physique of the Earl, the Captain looked old and short. His ragged ginger wig made him look a bit like a shaggy dog, or perhaps a small bear.

'Are you seriously telling me that this ridiculous old man is your second? I doubt if he could see far enough to hit a target. He is a perambulating wig.'

'Actually,' said Steve calmly. 'It's me. I'm the second. And by the way, since you challenged Liam to the duel we get to the chose the weapons. I'll be using the Captain's pistols.'

Earl Mostyn turned his attention to Steve.

'A boy?' he said incredulously. 'You'd let an idiotic boy like this take a bullet for you? The Countess of Shropshire would never marry a man like you. You're an absolute coward, Sir.'

'We've thought about it long and hard. It

turns out that I'm a very bad shot,' said Liam.
'Steve, on the other hand, can hit a flowerpot
on a sundial from a hundred yards.'

Rage flooded Earl Mostyn's veins. He was
a good shot, but the guns he'd prepared had
been loaded in his favour. His contained a
lead bullet. The one he was going to give
to Liam contained nothing but powder. He
took a step back as the Captain held out his
two pistols.

'Chose your weapon,' hissed the Captain.

'Wait,' said Earl Mostyn, 'if you are going to
fight with a second, then, surely, according
to the rules of duelling, I should also be
afforded the same luxury. Footman!'

The footman put down his cushion and
stepped forward.

'Kill this boy,' said Earl Mostyn, pointing
at Steve.

Steve smiled. He felt confident he could beat anybody in a duel.

'But…' stammered the footman.

'Go to it, man,' shouted Earl Mostyn.

'I will stand on the side and drop a handkerchief. First you must take a weapon. Then each of you must walk twenty paces apart. If Steve kills my footman, then we shall see who wins the heart of The Countess of Shropshire at the competition tonight. If, on the other hand, my footman kills Steve, then you forfeit your right to play any tunes to anybody.'

'Very well,' said Liam.

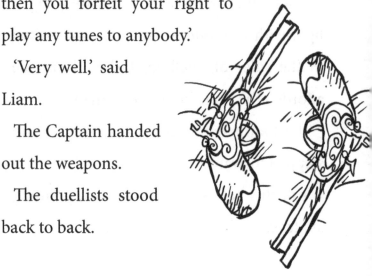

The Captain handed out the weapons.

The duellists stood back to back.

'One,' shouted the Captain.

They each took a pace away from one another.

'Two,' shouted the Captain.

Steve wasn't nervous at all. Duelling was fun.

'Three,' shouted the Captain.

'Go on, Steve,' urged Liam.

'Four,' said the Captain.

Steve and the footman took another step apart.

'Five.'

…and another.

As Steve and the footman stepped further apart, Earl Mostyn and Liam glared at one another.

Finally the Captain reached the end of the countdown.

'Twenty,' he cried as Earl Mostyn dropped a silk handkerchief. 'Duellists, you may turn and fire at will!'

Steve spun round. He was surprised to see the footman had already turned and was aiming the barrel of his gun directly at him. He saw a plume of smoke, he heard the loud bang of the powder and then he felt something whistle past his head.

Instinctively, Steve grabbed at his head. Then he looked at his hands. He expected to see blood pouring from a terrible head wound. But there was none. Then his wig landed on the grass near his feet. The footman had shot his wig off.

Liam and the Captain cheered.

'You missed!' they yelled.

'Now you have a free shot,' explained the Captain. 'The footman must stand still until you have blasted him to smithereens.'

Steve stared at the footman. A dreadful look of fear swept across the poor man's face.

'Go on Steve,' yelled The Captain, waving his crutch in the air. 'Blow his brains out.'

Steve stayed calm. He lined the barrel of his pistol up with the footman. He knew he had all the time in the world. Then he raised his gun high towards the sky and pulled the trigger. The bullet flew harmlessly upwards, narrowly missing a passing seagull.

The footman ran towards Steve, hugging him and thanking him for sparing his life. The Captain cursed old sailor's curses.

Earl Mostyn turned to Liam.

'Your fellow Steve is a man of honour,' he said.

Earl Mostyn jumped onto his black stallion.

'Honour has cost you The Countess of Shropshire,' he snarled. 'You have no music, no musicians and no chance of bringing an orchestra to the riverfront. This evening you'll watch the Countess choose me.'

As Earl Mostyn thundered off on his horse, Steve took the Captain to one side.

'We need to move quickly,' said Steve. 'You must know some musicians. Pirates are famous for their singing: hornpipes and reels, sea shanties and jigs.'

A smile flashed across the Captain's face.

'You mean like Cannonball Eric? Used to play his trumpet whenever we boarded a stricken vessel.'

'Exactly,' said Steve. 'We need every musician you can think of.'

'Jerry and the Sailmakers? The Hornpipe Hoochy Coochy Band? Bob Marley and the Whalers?'

'That's it,' said Steve, 'we'll beat their orchestra with musicians who've sailed the seven seas.'

The Captain told Steve where to find his old musicians and he gave him the names of the best ones. Then Liam and the Captain hurried away to set up the stage.

'I'll meet you at the riverfront at 7pm sharp,' yelled Steve.

10

Big Wigs

Steve burst into the Captain's cabin. There, exactly where Steve had left him, sat Wolfie, playing a wonderful tune on the keyboard. Steve gasped, almost in horror. Something was wrong. Wolfie was so engaged in the music he didn't hear Steve open the door. When Steve drew in his breath in shock Wolfie span round, reaching for his wig. He tried to hide his long, flowing red hair.

Steve stared at Wolfie.

'Errr,' he said.

Wolfie found the wig, tucked his hair under it and put it on his head.

'Hi, Steve,' said Wolfie, trying to pretend that everything was the same.

'You're a girl,' said Steve.

Wolfie smiled nervously.

'So?' she said.

Wolfie took the wig off.

Steve looked at Wolfie. Without the wig on, Steve could see that Wolfie was definitely a girl. She was older than him, maybe a bit older than Miffany. In fact, without the wig on, Wolfie looked very similar to Steve's sister Miffany.

Wolfie sighed and rested her elbows on the keyboard. A discordant sound roared from the harpsichord.

'That's it,' sighed Wolfie, 'we're done for. You'd better hand me over now.'

'What d'you mean?' asked Steve.

'Impersonating a boy is a punishable

offence,' said Wolfie, 'I could be put in prison.'

'Why?' asked Steve.

'What do you mean?' asked Wolfie. 'Why could I be sent to prison, or why am I impersonating a boy?'

'Both,' said Steve.

'Because I want to be a composer,' said Wolfie, 'and all the best composers are men. In fact, they don't allow women to be composers. They say that music has a strange effect on women and it turns them crazy.'

'That's ridiculous,' said Steve.

Then he remembered Mrs Gestetner his piano teacher. He thought about her death-ray eyes.

'Well,' he added, 'it's ridiculous in most cases. Girls are just as good at being composers as boys.'

Steve thought about his sisters. He remembered how they'd won the Pendown's Got Talent competition.

'Actually,' he said, 'in my experience, they're better.'

'Well, that makes you a very unusual boy,' said Wolfie. 'There's no way Liam's going to win the competition if they find out the music was written by a girl. And anyway, it's hopeless. We're going to need an orchestra — a string quartet at the very least.'

Steve tapped the top of the harpsichord with his conductor's baton.

'Play it, Wolfie,' said Steve. 'Let me hear the tune.'

Wolfie rested

her fingers on the harpsichord, then began to play. Now that she had an instrument that was in tune the music sounded wonderful.

When she finished Steve knew what to do.

'Put your wig back on,' said Steve. 'We're going to find ourselves an orchestra.'

Wolfie shoved her hair back under her wig. She put her old black coat on.

'And another thing,' said Steve. 'If we're going to win this competition we need to look the part. Look in the corner.'

Steve pointed at a coat stand. On it hung the Captain's most piratical jackets: a red one with sequins, a blue one with gold embroidery.

Steve took the red one. Wolfie put the blue one on.

'Now,' said Steve, 'can you take me to a tavern called The Cutlass and Snarl. The

Captain says it's the place to go to find his old crew and our musicians.'

A look of fear crossed Wolfie's face – her lip twitched.

'The Cutlass and Snarl?' she whispered.

'Yes,' said Steve. 'Is it far? We haven't got much time.'

'The problem with the Cutlass and Snarl,' said Wolfie, 'is this. It's full of murderers, pirates and thieves.'

'Good,' said Steve.

11

The Killer Singers

Steve followed Wolfie as she hurried along the thin cobbled streets. A distant clock chimed the hour.

'Come on, Steve,' shouted Wolfie. 'That's four bongs – you know what that means.'

'It's four o'clock?' suggested Steve, with just a hint of sarcasm in his voice. He stopped and lent on a door, getting his breath back.

'How much further?' asked Steve.

'Look above your head,' said Wolfie.

There was a sign above him. A man's head, bisected by a long scar that ran up his chin, along his nose and over his bald head, snarled out at them. Above him was a drawing of a sword.

'This is it,' said Wolfie. 'One cutlass, one snarl. That's the landlord: Twoface.'

They pushed the door open and stepped into a room crammed with people. Woodsmoke and chatter filled the air. In the background someone was scratching out a tune on an old violin. Steve and Wolfie began searching the room for musicians, but whenever they asked anyone if they knew the Captain, they were given the same answer.

'Never heard of 'im.'

After half an hour, Steve and Wolfie met at the fireplace.

'They've clammed up,' said Wolfie. 'They don't like strangers.'

Steve knew that they were running out of time. He put his hand inside his bright blue jacket. He felt the conductor's baton which the librarian had given him. He couldn't see how that would help. Then he felt the pistol the Captain had given him at the duel. He took a deep breath, then he pulled out the pistol, holding it straight out in front of him, pointing it at the people in the tavern.

Suddenly the babble of talking, singing 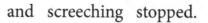 and screeching stopped. It was as if a cold wind had blown down the chimney into the room, snuffing out the sound in everyone's mouths.

Wolfie gasped.

'This is a blades pub,' she hissed. 'They don't like shooters.'

Steve gulped.

'OK everyone,' he said. 'Stick 'em up.'

Steve had never seen such an ugly-looking crew. Hard-bitten faces frowned down at him. Slowly the people in the tavern raised their arms high.

'What do you want?' a bald man behind the bar with a scar running straight down through the middle of his face, spoke for everyone. 'We got no money, we lost our treasure and you ain't no highwaymen.'

Steve didn't speak for moment.

'I want musicians,' he said, his voice faltering slightly.

Wolfie interrupted.

'A famous pirate, a friend of mine, well, not exactly a friend, more like a one-legged wig with a sword, known only as the Captain, has identified you as the top musical performers in the pirating business. If you can play a musical instrument the Captain needs help.'

Steve continued: 'He's given me some

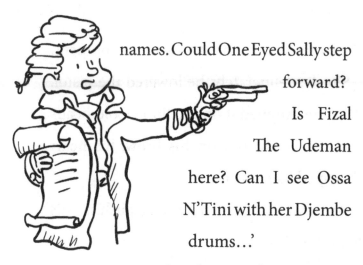

names. Could One Eyed Sally step forward?

Is Fizal The Udeman here? Can I see Ossa N'Tini with her Djembe drums...'

One by one the musicians came forward. A tall woman with long blonde hair and purple eyepatch spoke for them all.

'If the Captain's in trouble, we can help, but there's one thing — we don't allow pistols in this tavern. Put the gun down, boy.'

Steve gazed out at the sea of angry faces. He'd found his musicians. Now, it was up to them. If they wanted to kill him for breaking the rules of the Cutlass and Snarl, this was the moment.

Slowly, deliberately, he lowered the pistol. Then he dropped it on the floor. Cold beads of sweat stood out on his brow, his heart thumped like a drum.

'Are you with us?' he asked, pushing his hand into his jacket.

Everyone watched Steve as he produced another weapon from his jacket pocket. He held it high.

'This is my conductor's baton,' he said. 'Tonight we're playing for the Captain.'

The musicians cheered, but the bald man behind the bar of the old tavern stepped forward. He picked up the pistol and pointed it at Steve.

'Not so fast.'

Steve gulped and took a step back. But the man followed, pushing the pistol forward until the barrel rested on the tip of Steve's nose. Steve shook with fear. Everybody in the Cutlass and Snarl held their breath.

'We don't allow guns in the Cutlass and Snarl.'

Steve tried to speak, but he couldn't move his mouth. The cold steel of the barrel was making his nose feel numb. There was something about this man that scared Steve, it scared him to the heart of his dreams. What if he died in his dream? Big Mo wouldn't find him. He'd never get back to Pendown.

'You know my name?' said the man.

'Twoface?' breathed Steve.

'Not so stupid,' hissed Twoface. 'Just plain dumb. The penalty for bringing a handgun into the Cutlass and Snarl is death.'

Wolfie gulped. 'NO!' she shouted. 'You can't shoot him.'

'Wanna bet,' said the landlord, his face contorting into two menacing grins, separated from one another by that great scar that spliced his face.

Steve couldn't speak. All that would come out of his mouth was the first letter of the word 'Please'.

'P... p... p...'

He wanted to say, 'Please don't shoot me.' He thought about his mum, asleep in her bed in their house. He thought about Miffany and Jaydee, Groucho his little dog, even Kyled and Tobes. He missed them all and he wanted to go back to them. Tears filled his eyes. How had he dreamed himself into this terrible situation?

'P… p… p…'

Steve looked around him. He was surrounded by horrified, frightened faces.

He tried a new word.

'Help!' he screamed.

The musicians took a step back. Steve shut his eyes. His nose began to shiver. Slowly, Twoface tightened his grip on the trigger. He laughed as Steve winced in fear. He closed his eyes. This was it. He'd never get home.

Click.

Twoface pulled the trigger.

Snap.

The flint flicked to light the powder.

There was no explosion in the chamber. No crack and whizz as the lead ball flew out of the barrel.

The gun wasn't loaded.

Steve opened one eye. The same faces stared at him. He opened the other. He saw Twoface looking even more furious.

'Come on,' yelled Steve, 'follow me. Grab your instruments on the way. We'll practise on the old ship — *The Black Dragon*.'

Twoface made a grab for Steve, but he was too fast. As Steve and the others rushed away from the tavern he heard Twoface shouting after him, 'You can dream yourself anywhere, Steve, but wherever you go, whatever you try, I'll be there to stop you. I'll turn your dreams into nightmares.'

12

Rehearsals

A distant clock chimed. Steve and Wolfie counted the bongs.

'Six bongs,' muttered Steve as he shoved the harpsichord out onto the deck outside the Captain's cabin. 'We're almost out of bongs. It's going to be close but I think we can make it.'

'How?' moaned Wolfie, setting her stool down in front of the keyboard. 'The musicians don't know the tune and in case you hadn't noticed, we're on a run-aground ship on a mudflat miles from anywhere.'

Steve and Wolfie were standing on the raised deck just outside the Captain's cabin. A few metres below them stood the musicians on the bleached planks of the main deck. They didn't look impressive. They were dressed in rags and their instruments were old and battered. They were a crew of twangers, plinkers and plonkers drawn from the worst pirate ships that had sailed the seas.

Steve held up his conductor's baton.

'Ladies and gentlemen,' he cried. 'Let's give it up for the one and only … Wolfie.'

The musicians on the deck clapped without much enthusiasm. A seagull flapped down

and perched on a spar. It cocked its
head on one side.

Wolfie began to play. When she
finished, silence descended on the
ship like a quilt.

'It's good,' said Ossa. 'I can do something
with it.'

Sally picked up her violin and scratched a
note until her instrument was in tune with
Wolfie's. The others followed, tuning up
their instruments.

'This is going to sound terrible,' whispered
Wolfie.

'Why?' asked Steve, 'they all know their
instruments, they've heard your tune, I can't
really see what the problem is.'

'That's because you don't know anything
about music.'

A clock chimed. Wolfie and Steve listened.

Lots of bongs. It was half past six.

Steve took a deep breath and raised his baton skywards.

'I may not be so good at middle C,' he said, 'but when it comes to A, I'm on home ground. Now stop moaning, Wolfie – we've got one chance to get this right.'

Wolfie sat at the keyboard.

Steve tapped the mast with his baton.

The musicians on the deck fell silent, their instruments glinting in the setting sunlight. Steve felt their eyes zooming in on him. He realised that they weren't looking at his face. The tiny little stick in his hand was all they cared about. That was where the beat came from. Right now, Steve realised, his baton was as powerful as any wand. He jumped onto the balustrade between the captain's deck and the main deck and shouted at the top of his voice.

'A one, a two, a one, two, three, four…'

Steve spun around and pointed his baton at One Eye'd Sally. She played a scale on her violin and then introduced Wolfie's tune. Then Steve pointed to the other stringed instruments. They created a wonderful floating sound, less hard than Wolfie's harpsichord.

'OK,' cried Steve. 'Go now, Wolfie.'

Wolfie started playing. Steve kept the beat by tapping his feet and dancing around the deck swinging his baton through the air. Next he brought in the brass and woodwind players. Only then did he give Ossa N'Tini the nod. Bang! She hit the drum and got playing.

Steve danced all over the deck, tapping the musicians with his baton when he wanted them to play up or play down. As the song drew to a close, Steve found himself standing on top of Wolfie's keyboard, punching the air, shouting at the top of his voice.

'This is fantastic!'

But as the final chords died down and the sound rolled away along the river, Steve and Wolfie heard another, more worrying noise.

From a faraway tower a clock chimed the time.

Steve counted more bongs.

It was seven o'clock.

'Groovy,' said One Eye'd Sally.

'Dig it, man,' shouted Wolfie.

13

The Riverfront
Song Contest

Liam and the Captain had been busy. After the duel they'd hurried to the river and set to work putting out chairs for the audience. Nearby the Earl's servants had already constructed a stage and by the evening the best musicians in the country had taken up their positions.

Elegant couples arrived in carriages. Others strolled into the park on foot, clipping the floor with their brightly polished boots and canes. Everyone wanted to see who would win.

Earl Mostyn himself galloped in. He'd positioned a gold chair, a bit like a throne, on the side of the stage and he listened with pleasure as his conductor, his composer and his musicians began to rehearse his newly commissioned symphony.

Liam and the Captain sat on two of the wooden chairs they'd put out. They watched and listened.

The Captain spoke first as the orchestra crashed and surged through 'The Countess of Shropshire's First Symphony'.

'They're good, aren't they,' he said.

Liam nodded.

A huge white carriage pulled by four white stallions cantered up and stopped.

'I can guess who this is,' said the Captain. Liam watched as a beautiful woman in a bright blue dress with a huge, tall blueish wig stepped out of the carriage. Footmen ran before her, scattering blue petals on the ground in front of her.

'Look,' said Liam. 'Isn't she beautiful, like a great big blue cloud?'

'Clouds aren't blue,' said the Captain.

'It's the Countess of Shropshire,' sighed Liam. 'Isn't she wonderful?'

Liam waved towards the Countess. But she didn't notice. She walked towards Earl Mostyn's stage, smiling at him, his conductor, his orchestra and his audience.

'She's a looker and no mistake,' said the Captain.

'What a beautiful dress,' said Liam. 'It's so blue it makes the sky look boring.'

The Captain glanced up at the sky. The pink light of sunset was splodging across the walls of the nearby building. If anything it made the Countess' dress look almost purple.

'I'm not sure about the blue hair though,' said the Captain. 'I think that's a bit OTT.'

Liam was transfixed by the vision in blue as she processed towards the stage. The Earl leapt down from his stage and bowed. The Countess curtseyed. He took her hand and led her to a seat in the middle of the front row. All around, the audience gazed at the beautiful Countess. They adjusted their wigs. None of them had anything to compare with her incredible blue wig.

'Prepare to have your ears blown off,' said the Earl to the Countess.

She nodded graciously, flicking open a little blue fan which she kept folded on her wrist.

The band began to play. Their music was called 'A Symphony Inspired by the Radiance and Beauty of the Countess of Shropshire'. It was conducted by its composer, a small man wearing a white wig. His orchestra, all dressed in matching blue jackets and trousers were the best in the country.

When the Earl's orchestra finished playing, the entire audience stood to applaud. The orchestra leapt to their feet and saluted the Earl. The composer took a low bow and waved his wig at the cheering crowd.

The Countess stepped onto the stage.

'I had promised to marry the man who could express their love and appreciation of me the best in music,' she said. 'Earl Mostyn has certainly done that.'

She looked down at Liam and the Captain.

'Liam, on the other hand, has said nothing. Indeed, he has played nothing. Have you nothing to offer?'

Liam looked desperately from side to side. His stage was empty. The few seats that he and the Captain had managed to set up were also unoccupied. There was no sign of Wolfie and her harpsichord, let alone an orchestra. He knew he'd lost.

'I'm going to shoot myself,' he muttered.

'He'll probably miss,' said Earl Mostyn, leading the Countess of Shropshire away.

The Captain turned. Something had distracted him. He scanned the park, the buildings nearby, then the river.

'It is with great regret,' said Liam, 'that I…'

'Shut up,' said the Captain, poking Liam in the ribs with his crutch.

'Get on with it,' said the Earl. 'He's lost, I've won, let's get married, end of sports.'

'By thunder,' said the Captain, grabbing his wig and holding it down on his head, 'look at that!'

He pointed towards the river. Slowly, a black ship floated into view.

'She's coming up on the tide,' said the Captain. 'That's my old vessel, *The Black Dragon*. I didn't think she'd still float.'

'Yeah, but I don't see what that's got to

do with anything, we still haven't got an orchestra,' moaned Liam.

The ship creaked into view and sailed slowly towards the shore. It groaned in the wind as it drew closer and closer. The huge figurehead of a black dragon loomed towards the crowd. They gasped and hurried away as the ship ground into the mud.

Steve leapt onto the prow, evening sunlight sparkling on his bright red jacket.

'Ready?' he shouted, waggling

124

his baton in the air.

A cheer went up from within the ship.

'A one, a two, a one, two, three, four…'

The band began to play Wolfie's tune. They climbed the rigging, swung from the ropes, marched across the decks.

At first the audience didn't know what to do. But they couldn't help tapping their feet. Then they began to clap and cheer. Before long they were dancing. Musicians swung down to the ground on ropes. They filled the stage with their crazy dance, whilst Steve kept time with his baton. The harpsichord swung out over the crowd, and Wolfie kept playing as they lowered her down to the ground. Finally, at the end of the piece Steve pointed at the ship itself.

'Fire,' he shouted.

Cannons roared and smoke filled the

air. The audience, Liam, the Captain, Earl Mostyn's orchestra, Earl Mostyn, The Countess of Shropshire, the Earl's footman, even the Earl's great stallion, all threw themselves on the floor. Then, as the smoke cleared, they began to stand and cheer. Nobody had ever heard a piece of music like it before, and nobody heard anything like it ever again.

Steve grabbed Wolfie's hand and led her up onto the stage. She bowed and the crowd went wild, throwing their wigs into the air. Even the Countess of Shropshire smiled.

'It seems you have won the

competition,' she said, edging away from the Earl and towards Liam.

Liam bowed to the Countess.

The Earl stepped forward. He pulled Wolfie's wig off.

'I'm afraid this piece of music doesn't count for a start, it was written by a girl.'

The crowd gasped in horror.

'And half of that pirate band of desperados are girls too. It doesn't count.'

Liam looked at Wolfie standing by her harpsichord on the stage. He couldn't help thinking that her red hair looked much nicer than the Countess' blue wig.

Liam stepped away from the Countess.

In fact, he couldn't help thinking that Wolfie looked quite a lot prettier than the Countess, even though she didn't have a blue dress.

He stepped towards Wolfie.

'Do you always travel by airborne harpsichord?' asked Liam.

'I haven't got a carriage,' said Wolfie, leaping on top of her instrument, 'isn't this fantastic?'

'Play it again,' shouted the crowd.

The Earl threw his wig on the floor.

'Cheats!' he yelled.

'And anyway,' shouted the Earl,

'everybody knows girls can't be composers — whoever heard of music composed by a girl?'

Liam leaped onto the harpsichord and joined Wolfie.

'Me!' he cried. 'Three cheers for Wolfie.'

Steve rubbed his eyes. He felt strange. Wobbly. He tried to speak. But no sounds came out of his mouth. He tried to lift his hand, to wave his baton, but his fingers felt heavy, as if they were made of lead.

'Wait,' he cried. 'Wait! Wolfie! Liam! I don't want to go! Let me stay.'

Even the picture of the town was fading now. The huge sailing ship rammed up on the embankment with its black dragon figurehead glowering at the crowded riverside, began to break up, almost as if it was a jigsaw disintegrating as it fell to the ground. The wonderful stone buildings dissipated into grains of sand. Colours flickered on and off. Before Steve could say any more or reach out any further, it was gone. He found himself falling, head over heels. He was tumbling downwards, or was it upwards? He didn't suppose it mattered.

Steve screwed up his face. All he knew was that he was falling. And that meant one thing. At some point he'd stop falling. And that would hurt.

'Aaaaaaaaaaaaarrrrrgh,' yelled Steve.

Steve covered his face with his hands and pulled his knees up to his head. The wind rushed past his ears, filling his head with the sound of a thousand tornados.

14

Twoface

Then it stopped.

Steve   peeped
through his
fingers.

He saw the
librarian
smiling at him
from behind his desk.

Steve put his legs down. With some relief, he felt the floor. Instinctively, he pushed his hands forward and touched the front of the librarian's desk. It felt cool and solid. He tapped the oak legs. They felt heavy and strong.

'Sorry about that,' said a voice behind him. Steve saw big Mo, smiling from beneath his pork-pie hat.

'What happened?' spluttered Steve.

'Turbulence,' said Big Mo.

'We sometimes experience turbulence,' added the librarian, trying to sound as helpful as possible.

'If I could ask you to sign this form and return the conductor's baton, I'd be most grateful.'

Steve watched as the librarian pushed a piece of paper towards him.

'It's nothing special, just a formality.'

Steve read the top of the piece of paper: 'Return of Dream Equipment Loaned by the Library of Dreams'.

Steve stuck his hand in his pocket. He produced the conductor's baton and placed it carefully on the table.

'Was it useful?' asked the librarian.

'Totally,' said Steve. 'I could never have a conducted an orchestra without one.'

'Good work, Steve,' said Big Mo.

'What happened in the end?' asked Steve, as he signed the Return of Dream Equipment form.

'Didn't you see?'

'No,' said Steve, pushing the paper and the baton back to the librarian.

'It was a complete turnaround, what we in the business call a 180.'

Steve didn't quite understand.

'The Countess of Shropshire fell in love with Liam because he'd blown the Earl's boring orchestra out of the water. But guess what? Liam fell in in love with Wolfie because she was a genius, she was great fun and she looked great when she wasn't wearing a wig. You saved the day again, Steve,' said Big Mo.

'The Captain rejoined his crew and they sailed around the capital cities of Europe, with Liam and Wolfie putting on musical events from the decks of the old ship,' added the librarian. 'They really were happy ever after. And so were Earl Mostyn and the Countess.'

'I'm glad about that,' said Steve, handing his eighteenth-century clothes back to the librarian.

'See you next time,' said Big Mo. 'Thanks for your help, Steve.'

Steve smiled. He hurried back through the library and stepped out through the great arched door.

'No problem,' he said, as he jumped onto his roof and squeezed himself

back through the window into the top bunk. 'There was one thing though. I met this man – his name was Twoface. Who's he?'

But Big Mo had gone – the dream was over.

Steve sat next to Kyled who squeezed in next to Mum. The Riverfront concert hall in Newport was packed. The audience fell silent. The lights dimmed.

Shadowy figures hurried onto the stage. Steve heard four clicks. He mouthed the words, 'One, two, three, four', tapping his index finger like a baton.

The music started. The spotlights flashed over the stage and Jaydee and Miffany danced to the front of the stage each holding a microphone.

We are the Piratellas,
We sail the seas and blow up fellas.
We take their boats and steal their treasures,
And sing all day and dance all night.

Steve and Kyled sung along. All around the crowd clapped and cheered. Steve climbed onto his chair and waved his arms in the air. He was conducting again.